Does Anybody Love Me?

For Rachel G.L.
To Avril R.B.

Text copyright © 2002 Gillian Lobel
Illustrations copyright © 2002 Rosalind Beardshaw
Original edition published in English under the title *Does Anybody Love Me?* by Lion Publishing, plc,
Oxford, England. Copyright © Lion Publishing 2002.

North American edition published by Good Books, 2002. All rights reserved.

DOES ANYBODY LOVE ME?
Copyright © 2002 by Good Books, Intercourse, PA 17534
International Standard Book Number: 1-56148-368-0
Library of Congress Catalog Card Number: 2002024498

Printed and bound in Singapore.

Library of Congress Cataloging-in-Publication Data

Lobel, Gillian.
    Does anybody love me? / Gillian Lobel ; illustrated by Rosalind Beardshaw.
        p.cm.
    Originally published: Oxford, England : Lion Pub., 2002.
    Summary: Charlie runs away to a secret place in the back yard because she feels that her parents
do not love her, but her grandfather influences her to return home.
    ISBN: 1-56148-368-0
    [1. Runaways--Fiction. 2. Self-esteem--Fiction. 3. Grandfathers--Fiction.] I. Beardshaw, Rosalind,
ill. II. Title.

PZ7.L7798 Do 2002
[E]--dc21   2002024498

Does Anybody Love Me?

Gillian Lobel

Illustrated by
Rosalind Beardshaw

Good Books

Intercourse, PA 17534
800/762-7171
www.goodbks.com

Charlie was making chocolate pudding. She put some dark crumbly earth into the mixing bowl.

She added a handful of pebbles for raisins and a sprinkling of sand for sugar.

Then she went to the kitchen, turned on the cold water and watched her pudding go soft and squidgy.

She gave it a really good stir.

"Oh, Charlie!" Mom stuck her head around the door. "You've soaked the floor – and look at your socks! Not like my sensible girl at all."

"Nobody in this house loves me!" cried Charlie. She ran into her bedroom and threw herself on the bed.

"I'll run away," she said crossly. "Then they'll be sorry."

She took a little suitcase from under her bed. She put in a sweatshirt and a woolly hat. Then she picked up Panda and tucked him under her arm.

"We're going somewhere nice," she told him, "where there's no cross people."

Chocolate pudding flew all round the kitchen.

"Oh, Charlie! What a mess!"

Dad looked really cross. "That was a silly thing to do."

"I'm making chocolate pudding for Grandpa!" Charlie felt hurt.

"You're making a mess!" grumbled Dad.

Charlie stomped upstairs. She wouldn't give Dad any of her pudding.

She decided to play boats in the bathroom. She filled the washbowl full of water and sailed the bath-time boats around their little lake.

"Now there's a big storm coming!" She stirred the water hard. Little waves splashed over the soap.

"Crash!" She smacked the water hard for thunder. The waves rolled over the washbowl and poured onto the floor.

Charlie went into the
kitchen. She took some cookies
from the jar and a carton of juice
from the fridge. She squashed them
into her suitcase.

Then she went out the front
door.

She sat down on the front step.
Where should she go?
"I know. I'll run away to the
jungle. They'll never find me
there."

She went around to the back of the house. At the
bottom of the garden there was a dark tangle of laurel
bushes. You had to crawl through a little
tunnel to reach the secret hiding place.
The laurel leaves smelled sharp and
sweet. Silver cobwebs stuck to her
hair and pinged her nose
softly.

Then she was there, at her favorite place. You couldn't see the house at all. Tall fir trees made a secret den where their branches bent low to the ground, and in the corner there was a tumble of little rocks.

She crept through the curtain of shivering fir.

"Now we'll have a party," she told Panda.

They shared the cookies and the juice.

Then they played shipwreck. Charlie was the captain, and Panda was the ship's monkey. Charlie splashed through the green waves, holding Panda safely out of the water, until she reached a desert island.

"We must find water," she cried. They sat down and pretended to drink.

It was fun, but she was really thirsty now. There was no more juice in the carton, and Panda was beginning to whimper.

Suddenly a drop of water landed on her hand.

"It's raining!" shouted Charlie. "We're saved, Panda!"
She stuck out her tongue to catch the drops. The rain was
warm and sweet, but not enough.

It got very dark under the fir trees. Charlie shivered.

"Don't worry, Panda," she said.
"I'll look after you."

Rain trickled down the back
of her neck, and her skin went
cold and bumpy.

Suddenly there was a flash of lightning. Charlie grabbed Panda and held him tight.

"I want to go home!" shouted Panda.

"We can't," said Charlie.

"Nobody loves us anymore."

In the bushes something crackled. The noise got closer. Twigs snapped, and Charlie could hear breathing!

Then a head stuck through the secret passage.
It was Grandpa's.

"Oh, Charlie," he panted. "I'm so glad I've found you – I'm lost in the jungle, and I don't know how to find my way home!"

"Don't worry, Grandpa." Charlie hugged him tightly. "I'll save you – just follow me!"

She and Panda took
Grandpa all the
way home.
"Oh, thank
goodness you've
found Grandpa!" said
Mom, giving her a hug. "That's my brave girl!"

Then Charlie led Grandpa into the warm kitchen and
gave him a lovely big helping of chocolate
pudding.